The Invisible Man

Arthur Yorinks

Illustrated by **Doug Cushman**

HARPER

An Imprint of HarperCollinsPublishers

For Mark, Jeanette, Jeremy, and Jane
—A.Y.

To Sally and Martha,
with no invisible thanks
—D.C.

Library of Congress Cataloging-in-Publication Data
Yorinks, Arthur.
        The invisible man / by Arthur Yorinks ; illustrated by Doug Cushman. — 1st ed.
            p.   cm.
        Summary: Sy Kravitz, a Brooklyn fruit seller, explains why becoming invisible should never happen to
you.
        ISBN 978-0-06-156148-1 (trade bdg.) — ISBN 978-0-06-156149-8 (lib. bdg.)
        [1. Supernatural—Fiction.   2. Humorous stories.]   I. Cushman, Doug, ill.   II. Title.
PZ7.Y819In   2010   2009001404
[E]—dc22   CIP
                                                                                                                AC
Typography by Dana Fritts
11 12 13 14 15   SCP   10 9 8 7 6 5 4 3 2 1   ❖ First Edition

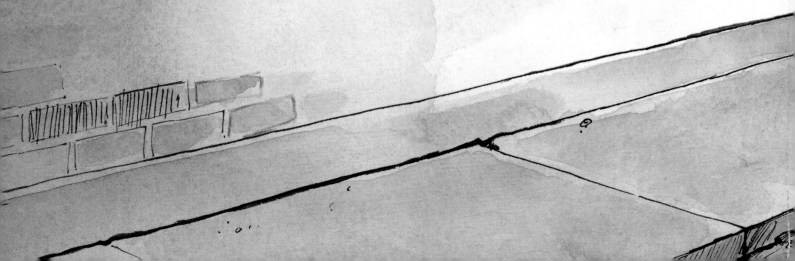

Sy sold fruit. Peaches. Plums. Pears. At a stand on Pitkin Avenue, Sy Kravitz catered to his customers.

"Sy, I have such a headache," Mrs. Schwartz complained.

"A headache? Take a nectarine," said Sy.

"Oh, my aching feet!" Mr. Maloney moaned.

"Bananas," Sy advised. "One banana and your feet will thank you."

Backaches, bunions, fevers, or fits. Day and night, with lines around the block, Sy helped everyone. He was kind. He was caring. And, what else, he knew fruit.

So tell me. What kind of world is it that one day this nice Sy Kravitz, without warning, disappeared!

It all started on August twenty-first. That morning, after an especially invigorating shower, Sy glanced in the mirror.

"Hmm," he said to himself. "I look a little pale. All right. I'll eat a few prunes and tomorrow I'll be tip-top."

But the next day Sy was not tip-top.

He was invisible.

Worried, Sy went to his doctor, Dr. Ludemann.
"Well?" Sy asked as the doctor examined him.

"I don't see anything wrong with you, my friend," Dr. Ludemann informed him. "Of course, I don't see you at all. Perhaps you should visit a specialist."

Sy went to doctor after doctor. But no one could help him. No one. Sy didn't know where to turn. "Maybe if I go to work, it will pass."

It didn't.

Ceil from Canarsie, a regular customer, said, "If there's nothing wrong with his fruit, why is he so ashamed to show his face?"

Rumors about Sy's merchandise began to fly, and soon even his best customers stayed away. Sy became nervous and irritable. "If they don't want my fruit," he declared, "let them eat cake!"

Life was miserable for Sy Kravitz. He was
shunned. Ignored. Alone and invisible, his gentle
spirit finally snapped. "I'll show them!" he cried.
"I'll show them!"

And he did. He snuck into movie theaters and rode the train for free. He slipped into the opera and expensive shows. He even stole onto a cruise.

"Invisible?" Sy mused. "Ha! It could be worse."

Unfortunately, it got worse. On a jet returning from London, Sy, forgetting himself, made the mistake of asking for extra peanuts. This caused a sensation.

News of the existence of an invisible man exploded, and suddenly there were sightings everywhere. In Rome. In Egypt. In Nova Scotia. It wasn't long before every unexplainable occurrence, every accident, every tragedy in life was blamed on the invisible man. For crimes he never committed, Sy Kravitz was hunted worldwide.

To elude capture, Sy took on various disguises.

Brain surgeon.

Pizza chef.

Scuba diver.

In this demeaning way, he kept one step ahead of
the authorities. Yet it could not last. It did not last.

One fateful night, desperate, hungry, and tired of pretending to be someone else, Sy snuck into a donut shop and stole a donut. A powdered donut. As the sugar flew, Sy the invisible man was finally caught.

"It was just a donut!" Sy pleaded at his trial. But it was no use. Sy was convicted of numerous offenses he had nothing to do with.

Years passed and the invisible man, away in jail,
was ultimately forgotten.

His time served, Sy took the only job available to him: a magician's assistant.

At the Pines Hotel, as Manny the Terrific waved his wand, Sy Kravitz vanished. Every night and twice on Sundays, it always worked like a charm.

Well, almost always.

One night, as they performed for a rowdy group of
people on diets, a man yelled out, "It's a trick. It's a fake!"
Suddenly the entire hungry audience, not pleased with
the performance, or maybe their dessert, began throwing
assorted fruit.

"Help!" yelled Manny. Sy, without thinking, stood in front of the magician and, ever the fruit salesman, called out, "Please, don't throw the good ones." But they did. They even threw the melon out of season.

And then it happened. A miracle. Covered in fruit cocktail, Sy Kravitz regained his color. There was his head. His arms. His legs. He was visible! He was a visible man again! Everyone leaped to their feet, applauding.

"I love fruit," a tearful Sy told the appreciative crowd.

Time, and fruit, heals all wounds.